Winter Wishes

With Christmas wishes for my god-daughters
Madeline Calthrop and Daisy Brett
Love Auntie Emma xx

Emma Thomson's
felicity Wishes®

FELICITY WISHES
Felicity Wishes © 2000 Emma Thomson
Licensed by White Lion Publishing

Text and Illustrations © 2006 Emma Thomson

First published in Great Britain in 2006 by Hodder Children's Books

A Catalogue record for this book is available from the British Library.

ISBN-10: 0340 911999
ISBN-13: 9780340911990

Printed in Hong Kong by Sheck Wah Tong Printing Press Ltd

Hodder Children's Books
A division of Hachette Children's Books, 338 Euston Road, London NW1 3BH

Emma Thomson's

felicity Wishes ®

Winter Wishes

and other stories

h
Hodder
Children's
Books

A division of Hachette Children's Books

How to *make your Felicity wishes*

WISH

With this book comes an extra special wish
for you and your best friend.

Hold the book together at each end and
both close your eyes.

Wriggle your noses and think of a
number under ten.

Open your eyes, whisper the numbers you
thought of to each other.

Add these numbers together. This is your

Magic Number.

you

best
friend

Place your little finger
on the stars, and say your magic number
out loud together. Now make your wish
quietly to yourselves. And maybe, one day,
your wish might just come true.

Love *felicity* x

CONTENTS

Festive Fun

Festive Fun

Felicity Wishes' friend Daisy had been growing something very special. For years now the fir tree that stood in the best spot in her garden had been sprouting new branches and bursting with new needles. Over the summer, Daisy's tree had grown almost a wand-length in height!

The fir tree wasn't like any other tree. It literally glittered with magic. If you touched its branches, even on a rainy day, it would fill you with

happy feelings. And there was one special reason it could do this. Daisy's fir tree was a Christmas tree, the most magical tree that grew in Fairy World.

Each year, twelve days before Christmas Day, Daisy and her friends Felicity, Holly, Polly and Winnie prepared the tree for the time of year it glittered most.

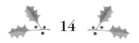

"I can't believe how much it's grown!" said Felicity, puffing as she brushed her hair out of her eyes. They were getting ready to fly the tree to the School of Nine Wishes.

"It's taller than me now," said Daisy, feeling nostalgic. "Can you remember when it was so tiny it only took two of us to fly it into school?"

"Yes, there are photos of all of us standing next to it on the last day of term, and you can barely see its star!" remembered Felicity.

"One day," said Holly, proudly heaving her side of the pot into the air, "it will be big enough for me to stand on top!"

"Do you still want to be a Christmas Tree Fairy when you graduate?" asked Felicity.

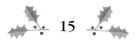

"I've never wanted to be anything else!" said Holly. "What could be more special?"

And as the five fairy friends wobbled off into the sky, none of them at that moment could think of anything more special than being a Christmas Tree Fairy.

When they got to school there was already a crowd of fairies waiting for them. The arrival of the Christmas tree had become a bit of an event.

"Here it comes!" announced Fairy Godmother, who couldn't disguise her own excitement. With each year that passed, all the fairies' love for the tree had grown.

"Stand back, let the fairies set it down carefully."

And in the middle of the crowd a clearing was made and Felicity, Holly, Polly, Daisy and Winnie carefully lowered the tree, with expert wing control.

* * *

This year would be extra special for the tree. Fairy Godmother had organized something that the whole

school could be part of.

"I don't mind at all," said Daisy when Fairy Godmother had asked for her thoughts. "My friends and I have always decorated it in the past without even thinking about whether anyone else might like to help."

"I'm glad you agree," said Fairy Godmother. "It would be lovely if everyone could decorate it. The Christmas tree is growing more magical each year and I think it would be a wonderful way to put that magic to good use."

* * *

The next morning in assembly Fairy Godmother brought a large red sack on to the stage. As she started her speech, she pulled out a small silver box and held it high above her head.

Felicity was already tingling at the thought of Christmas, and now nearly burst with anticipation.

"In my sack here," Fairy Godmother began, "I have a little silver box for each and every one of you."

And she showed them a little tag with a fairy's name written on it.

The hall of fairies erupted into a spontaneous cheer.

"Oh, no! Oh, no!" laughed Fairy Godmother, waving her arms to calm the crowd. "It's not what you think. These boxes don't contain presents for you!"

The hall fell silent.

"They're far more exciting than that!" said Fairy Godmother, not wanting to disappoint her students. She took off the lid to show them. "They're empty!"

Confused fairies looked up at Fairy Godmother.

"And I'd like you to fill them. Place inside the most magical gift you can think of for the person who it's

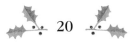

addressed to. Don't put your name on the box, though, and don't tell anyone else. It's a secret! The most exciting part about this present is that it isn't from you. It's from the Christmas tree!"

Felicity and her friends had never heard of anything like this before.

"An anonymous Christmas present?" said Holly, a little confused.

"How will we know who to thank?" said Polly sensibly.

"The tree!" said Felicity, who was beside herself with excitement. "The tree is giving gifts to all of us!"

* * *

For the next week every single fairy at the School of Nine Wishes was consumed with finding ideal presents. They had each chosen a box from

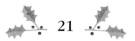

Fairy Godmother's big red bag, and couldn't stop thinking about the fairy whose name was on their box.

"I'm sure you've got Felicity for your Christmas tree present," whispered Holly, peeping over Polly's shoulder as Polly tried very hard to see if she could fit a pair of pink tights into the little package.

"No!" said Polly, blushing, then added, "What makes you say that?

There's more than one Felicity in this school, anyway."

"But there's only one Felicity Wishes who likes everything pink!" Holly giggled. She put her own box on the table and frowned at it.

"Who have you got to fill your box for?" asked Daisy.

"You know we can't tell!" said Holly, looking doubtfully at the label. "But even if I could tell, it wouldn't matter. Even I don't know who it is. I've never met them."

"Then how will you know what they'd like to receive?" asked Winnie.

"I won't!" said Holly. "And that's exactly why I haven't found anything to put inside it yet."

Suddenly, Felicity had a brainwave. "I've just had a thought. If we're

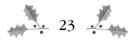

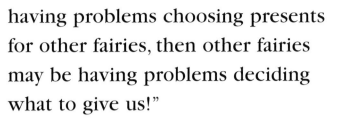

having problems choosing presents for other fairies, then other fairies may be having problems deciding what to give us!"

"Oh, goodness!" said Daisy. "Present-opening day is going to be fun!"

"Or disastrous!" added Holly, who had never forgotten the year Felicity had given them all badly knitted wand warmers.

"That's exactly why we have to help other fairies and show them what we like and what we don't!" offered Felicity.

"And," said Polly sensibly, "make an effort to find out what the person we have to fill our box for likes and doesn't like."

* * *

So for the week that followed Felicity, Daisy, Polly, Winnie and Holly behaved very strangely indeed! Not only were they being more vocal than ever about what they did and didn't like, but they were also secretly monitoring the fairies whose names appeared on their tag.

"Would you like potato with that?" said the School Dinner Fairy to Felicity as she held out her plate.

"Oh, yes!" said Felicity, rather too loudly. "I LOVE potato. I also love SWEETS. If anyone was thinking of giving me a present, SWEETS would be very welcome."

The dinner fairy looked at Felicity as if she was mad.

"Sorry, did you say yes to potato? If you want puddings they're down

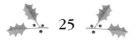

25

the other end." And she waved her spoon in the other direction.

As Felicity sat down with her lunch her foot bumped something under the table. As she crouched to move what she thought was someone's school bag, she saw that it was Polly.

"What are you doing down there?" burst out Felicity.

"Sssssshhhh!" said Polly firmly. "I'm secretly watching the fairy whose

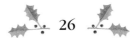

name is on my Christmas box."

Felicity looked over to the fairy in question, who appeared to be having problems getting her pen to work.

"You mean, you've got Sarah in the year below us?" she asked, knowing Polly wouldn't be able to say.

Polly looked awkwardly up at Felicity, then returned to staring intently.

"You do know there are three Sarahs in the school, don't you?" offered Felicity unhelpfully.

Polly gave up trying to hide. Felicity had caused too much unwanted attention! Pulling her wings straight and brushing herself down, Polly shuffled on to the bench next to her friend.

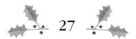

"Oh, Felicity," she moaned. "Look, I've made a hole in my tights."

"YOU'D REALLY LIKE A NEW PAIR OF TIGHTS THEN, POLLY?" shouted Felicity, not looking at her friend but at all the fairies that were sharing the table with them.

"YES!" said Polly. "A NEW PAIR OF TIGHTS WOULD BE A WONDERFUL PRESENT TO GIVE ME. Good thinking, Felicity," she said more quietly.

* * *

Holly was having worse luck than Polly. She thought she'd done well tracking down the fairy called Tabitha whose name was on her box, and she thought she'd done even better when she saw how badly Tabitha needed a hairbrush. But it all went horribly wrong! Holly was just about to pick up a very clever foldaway hairbrush that would fit into the silver box when the checkout assistant called to her supervisor.

"The silver sparkly hairbrush that was ordered in for Tabitha at the School of Nine Wishes has arrived. Shall I give her a ring to let her know?"

Holly was devastated. She couldn't believe her ears. The compact hairbrush had been such a good idea.

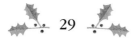

The perfect present! So perfect, she realized she'd actually quite like one herself.

* * *

Meanwhile, Winnie was fretting. Letting your likes and dislikes known

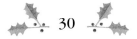

to everyone who could hear wasn't something she was getting used to.

"The thing is, Winnie," said Felicity when she found out about the problem, "you're so easy-going that you don't dislike anything!"

"It's true!" admitted Winnie. "I've tried to make sure everyone knows what I like. But when I found myself enthusing about the laces on my walking boots, I really began to worry! They're practical, but I'd prefer a more exciting Christmas gift!"

* * *

Daisy was sure that she'd found the fairy whose name was on her box. There was only one Philomena in the

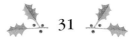

school. The trouble was, she was at home poorly. All her friends were into dancing, but Daisy couldn't be sure that Philomena enjoyed the same things as her friends. After all, Daisy knew that none of her best friends loved flowers the way she did. She was going to have to think of the perfect Christmas gift for any fairy, especially a poorly one!

* * *

The week came to an end and Felicity, Winnie, Holly, Polly and Daisy met by the library steps on Star Street. It was the last shopping day before the Christmas tree was decorated with their filled silver boxes.

It took them all day, and many changed minds and indecisions, but finally they finished. Each of them

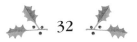

glowed with pride that night,
confident that they had chosen a gift
that would suit any fairy. In fact,
each of their gifts was so lovely that
even they themselves might like to
receive it.

At last the day came. The Christmas
tree looked dazzling, with more than
a hundred tiny silver boxes resting
in its branches and gathered around
its base. Everyone could see that
Christmas really was here, and
Felicity in particular couldn't contain
her excitement.

Every single fairy in the school
surrounded the tree, which glowed
with magic in the winter afternoon
dark. But as Fairy Godmother arrived,
the end of her wand lighting up the
sky as she hovered above the tree,

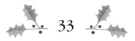

shocked gasps echoed from fairies'
mouths. Something magical had
happened to the presents that
decorated the tree. The small
silver gift boxes were
no longer silver...
they were gold!

"Fairies," began
Fairy Godmother,
addressing the crowd.
"The boxes you placed
on this tree have gone
on a magical journey. The
names on the tags attached to those
presents were not for the fairy friends
that surround you now, but for the
fairies at your twin school in Lower
Lucky. These golden boxes are their
presents for you, given with the gift
of Christmas which has only been
made possible by this wonderful
magical tree!"

"No wonder we had such a hard

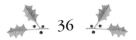

time trying to work out who our presents were for!" whispered Polly to Felicity.

And as each of the fairies carefully undid the ribbon on their small golden gift they couldn't believe their eyes! Each of them had been given the gift they had most secretly wished for! And the magic was that the presents they received were almost identical to what they had each given!

Polly unwrapped a new pair of tights, Felicity received a bag of her favourite sweets, Holly got a fabulous foldaway hairbrush, Winnie received a magic pair of self-tying laces and Daisy was speechless when she unwrapped a small pot of the rarest snowdrops.

"Now that's magic…" said Felicity, looking lovingly up at the tree, "…the true magic of Christmas!"

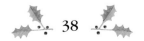

Put magical love
into what you give

and it will always
be returned

Winter Wishes

The fairies at Lower Lucky school invite you and four friends to a Christmas party tonight.

Winter Wishes

Felicity was in ecstasy! She loved surprises and this Christmas was full of them. As she opened up her golden Christmas tree gift, she could hardly believe her luck.

Sweeties were one of Felicity's favourite things. But as she took away the twinkly top wrapper of the present, she found something that made her eyes sparkle even more than the chocolates inside.

"Look!" she said, showing her box

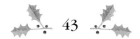

to Holly, Polly, Daisy and Winnie. "It's a letter!" She hastily pulled it out and held it up to read in the dark of the winter sky.

"It's not a letter, it's an invitation! An invitation to a Christmas party for me and four friends at our twin school in Lower Lucky – tonight!"

Each of the fairy friends had been given a wonderful present, but Felicity's was certainly the most exciting.

"We've no time to go home and get changed!" said Winnie, studying the invitation more closely. "If we're to get there on time, we'll have to leave at once. Flying won't be easy in this wind."

Felicity was in her element. She loved to do things on the spur of the moment. Her best friend Polly, however, was almost entirely the opposite.

"The weather reports are dreadful," she warned. "I'm really not sure it's sensible to embark on a long flight if there might be a storm."

"Oh, where's your sense of Christmas fun?" moaned Holly, who was more concerned about having a good time and was already warming up her wings.

Polly shrugged. Holly was right – it's not every day of the year you get

invited to a fairy Christmas party
by your twin school!

* * *

The five fairy friends
hadn't been flying long
before thick white
snow clouds began to
drift on to their path.
Within minutes they were
winging their way through a
blizzard.

"I'm so glad I'm wearing my
snow goggles!" called Felicity.

"I'm just pleased we all
wrapped up extra warm before
we left," Polly replied.

"My new Christmas hairbrush
is going to come in very handy
when we get there!" came a
voice from inside the cloud itself.

"Holly?" shouted Felicity.
"Where are you?"
But Felicity didn't
hear the reply.
Suddenly an
enormous billowing
wind swept all the
fairies up into the air
and tossed them around
in a mass of snowflakes.
"This is like being in
one of those toy snow
globes!" shrieked Felicity,
but none of her friends
could hear her.
The wind blew,

clouds tumbled, snowflakes whirled, and inside it all the five fairy friends squealed. Desperate to find something or someone to cling on to, Felicity flung out her arms. At exactly the same time the end of a fairy wand became visible for a second, just in time for Felicity to take hold of it.

"Winnie?" said Felicity as she took hold with two hands and grappled to find a hand to grasp. "Polly? Daisy?" she shouted into the washing-machine sky. "Holly?"

But as Felicity pulled herself closer to the fairy whose hand she held, she saw it wasn't any of her friends. Even in the hazy whirl of snowflakes, Felicity could see that it was a fairy she had never met before.

Felicity wasn't the only one who

had bumped into a stranger in the sky. Holly had managed to stabilize herself by linking arms with two new fairy friends. Polly had found her legs locked in a tangle of wings, and Winnie and Daisy thought they were holding on to each other until they realized there was someone between them!

* * *

When the blustery snow clouds finally parted and the blizzard died down, the group of fairies began an unsteady descent to the ground.

"Let me introduce myself and my friends!" said Felicity, as the fairies separated themselves out. "We're all from the School of Nine Wishes and we're on our way over to our sister school in Lower Lucky for a Christmas party. This is Winnie, Holly, Polly and Daisy."

"How funny!" said one of the other fairies, coming forward. "We were on our way to Lower Lucky for the party too. But I'm afraid there won't be much of a party without us."

Holly looked shocked. She loved to be the centre of attention at a party, but even she wasn't bold enough to suggest that it wouldn't be a party without her there!

"We were driving the van with all the party equipment in it, and it broke down," explained another of the fairies. "We had to fly for help – but we ended up getting caught in that dreadful storm, where we bumped into you."

"This is Abby, Kate, Cecily, and I'm Miranda," said the fairy who had spoken first.

"So where's your van and all the party equipment now?" asked Felicity, looking around her.

"Your guess is as good as ours!" said Cecily desperately. "It can't be too far – we were only in the air for a few minutes before the storm struck."

Everyone looked blankly around them. They were standing in the middle of a large snow-covered field, and it was impossible to know where anything was. The snow itself had calmed to a gentle flurry, but all of them could see that the clouds were not far away.

"What shall we do?" said Felicity, looking helplessly at the sky. Any Christmassy feelings she'd had before they'd left were well and truly gone now.

Polly and Miranda immediately took charge.

"Some of us should stay here, and a couple of us should try to get to the school and let them know what's happened," said Polly.

Felicity jumped at the chance to help out. "I'll fly off to the school and see if I can find our new friends!"

Polly looked at her a little dubiously. Felicity wasn't known for her good sense of direction! But once she saw that Miranda would go with Felicity, she knew they'd be all right. "I'll stay here, then," she said, "and help Winnie find some shelter close by."

Felicity and Miranda took to the sky, while Winnie had already got her compass out. When Winnie graduated she wanted to become an Adventure

Fairy, and being put in charge of finding shelter was a wonderful and unexpected Christmas present.

"Right," she said, looking serious and gazing intently up at the stars. "I know exactly where we are, but just not in reference to anywhere else."

"What does that mean?" said Holly, whose toes were getting cold.

"Basically, I know how to get us back to this spot if we get lost looking for shelter."

Polly, Holly, Daisy, Abby, Kate and Cecily exchanged looks. None of them was in the mood for getting even more lost than they already were.

"Trust me," said Winnie earnestly. "You see that large sparkling star? The big one next to the two little ones?"

The fairies looked up and nodded.

"Well, we're directly under that,"
said Winnie. "Come on - let's get
looking!"

None of the fairies really wanted to
follow Winnie, but they all knew that
if they didn't their wings would be in

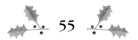

"This is impossible!" said Cecily. "Once you get below the surface, the snow is rock hard."

"So hard it feels like metal!" agreed Abby.

"Scrape sharply with the edge of your star," suggested Winnie. "It should start to break up."

"Nope," said Daisy, who was almost in tears.

Winnie came over to where they were digging. "Let me show you," she suggested, trying to keep their morale up.

But as Winnie tried to scratch into the icy-hard snow with the edge of her star, the wand pinged off completely!

"You're right," said Winnie, who narrowly managed to dodge the flying star as it whizzed past her head. "It's as hard as metal."

Suddenly, Polly bounced up behind them.

"That's because it is metal!" she burst out. "This isn't a hill we're trying to dig a hole in. It's the party van, buried by the snow!" And with a forceful sweep of her wand she exposed the edge of one of the doors.

Kate, Cecily and Abby began clearing now with a passionate energy… because they knew what was inside. In less than an hour the doors were completely cleared of snow.

Felicity and Miranda had had a tough flight. They'd been flying in the direction of Lower Lucky for some time when the storm that they'd escaped only a short time earlier swept them up again. This time it was worse. Neither Felicity nor Miranda could see anything except white before their eyes, as they were once more tossed amongst the snow clouds like clothes in a washing machine.

Holding on to Miranda's hands tightly, Felicity called out to her new friend, "I think I'm going to faint! I can see stars before my eyes!"

"So can I!" Miranda replied. She could see flickering golden specks all around her.

Before either of them could work out what was happening, they were

suddenly completely surrounded by
dozens of fairies with golden sparkling
starred wands raised high above them.
Within moments, the fairies had
created a protective circular barrier
against the elements with their wings
and Felicity and Miranda were able
to hover comfortably inside.

"We came as soon as we heard the storm was breaking," said the head fairy, who had long blonde hair just like Fairy Godmother. "Are you fairies from Fairy Parties Unlimited or from the School of Nine Wishes?"

Felicity and Miranda were astonished.

"Both," said Felicity, calling into the wind. "But how did you know?"

"We're from Nine Wishes' twin school in Lower Lucky. We've been expecting you – but we thought we'd find more than two fairies!"

"There are lots more of us, but we left them behind to find shelter," said Felicity.

"But there's no shelter for miles," said the head fairy, with a note of urgency in her voice. "Can you take

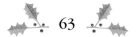

63

us to where you left them? There may still be time to get to them before their wings freeze."

Miranda's sense of direction was better than Felicity's, so they easily led the rescuing fairies to exactly where they could find their freezing friends.

But as they neared, none of the fairies could see evidence of anyone. Felicity was filled with dread, and regret that she hadn't stayed to help.

Just then, the head fairy from Lower Lucky called out from the front.

"I can see something!" she cried. "It looks like a distress flare. They must have spotted us and let it off to guide us to them."

Felicity frowned as she flew. She knew Winnie was a very keen

Adventure Fairy, but having a handy distress flare in her pocket was, she thought, very unlikely. Suddenly, there was a huge bang and the sky lit up with a million beautiful lavender-blue stars.

"That's not a distress flare," cried Felicity. "It's fireworks!"

When Felicity, Miranda and their new friends landed, all the Christmas magic suddenly returned to their hearts.

There in the middle of the snow-covered field was the most magical Christmas party!

Most of the fairies didn't even take off their coats before they joined in the dancing, chatting and giggling. It was going to be a night to remember!

* * *

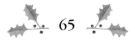

"Thank you for inviting us all to your
Christmas party!" said Daisy when

Felicity introduced her to the head fairy.
"I'm sorry we got here before you!"

The head fairy giggled. "There was rather an unexpected change of venue at the last moment! I'm just glad everyone made it… into a magical Christmas party that we'll never forget!"

And a large firework of stars filled the sky.

Some of the most
memorable magic moments

can arrive out of
unexpected disasters!

Snowy Surprise

Snowy Surprise

It was Christmas Eve. Felicity and her friends Holly, Polly, Daisy and Winnie had had a wonderful Christmas so far. They'd helped decorate the most magical Christmas tree, given and received fantastic presents, and they'd even been on a snow-swept adventure that had ended in an enormous fairy Christmas party under the stars.

None of them could quite believe there would be more Christmas magic yet to come, but there was. That

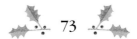

evening the whole of Little Blossoming would be gathering at the top of Star Street to sing carols by candlelight. It was the time Felicity loved most at Christmas and she could hardly wait.

* * *

That afternoon, after each of the fairies had finished wrapping the last of her presents, Felicity and her friends met outside Sparkles, the café on the corner. But it wasn't to spend the usual hours gossiping over hot chocolate. They'd met because they'd decided to spread some Christmas magic. The fairies were flying off on a mission.

"How did you get the idea?" asked Polly as she flapped to catch up with Felicity.

"There was an article in *The Daily*

Flutter about fairies who lived outside town getting cut off around this time of year because of all the snow," Felicity replied, wobbling a little as she rummaged around in her pocket to show her friend the cutting.

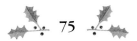

The Daily Flutter

COLD FAIRIES CUT OFF FOR WINTER

Owing to an unexpected blizzard, fairies living on an island in the middle of a lake close to the town of Little Blossoming have found themselves in a lonely predicament this Christmas. Their boats are frozen and all the wing power they have is being used for keeping warm, so getting into town for the usual festive treats will be something these fairies will have to miss this year.

"Are you sure that performing our Christmas pantomime on ice will cheer them up?" asked Daisy as she flew in alongside them.

"Positive!" said Felicity – who knew they'd literally have a captive audience!

But as the fairy friends flew closer to the lake, Daisy became less sure. "I can't see a single fairy!" she said

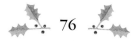

as she peered across to the island through the snow.

"You'd be inside too if you lived here!" said Holly, who hadn't been that keen on coming, even if it was to spread some Christmas magic.

"We should land here and skate across," said Polly sensibly. "We can't risk our wings freezing as we fly over the lake. If we landed on the ice from this height we'd fall through it into the freezing water, before anyone could wave their wand!"

As the fairy friends descended close to the lake's edge they could finally see firsthand what the papers had reported. Over at the island, the boats that were usually used to cross to the mainland were stuck fast in the ice and filled with snow!

"Poor them!" said Winnie, tying the laces of her skates.

"They probably don't even have a Christmas tree," said Polly.

"And they've missed out on everything Christmassy that's happened in Little Blossoming," said Holly, pulling

a long glittery piece of tinsel from her
bag and flinging it round her neck
like a scarf.

"Well," said Felicity, jumping on to
the ice, "we're about to change all
that, and bring Christmas to them!"

Giggling in the cold night air, Felicity, Holly, Polly, Daisy and Winnie skated arm in arm all the way across the lake until they reached the island. There was still no sign of anyone when they got there. But as Holly took off her skates and replaced them with her snow boots she heard a long low squeal.

"What was that?" she said to the others. "Did anyone else hear it?"

And just as they all stopped what they were doing to listen more carefully, there was an enormous shrieking noise that sounded like dozens of fairies all screaming at once. Then it went quiet.

aaahhh!

aaahhh!

aaahhh!

aaahhh!

aaahhh!

aaahhh!

"I don't like the sound of that!" said Daisy anxiously.

"I hope they're all OK," said Felicity.

"Perhaps we should bring them some Christmas spirit another time," offered Holly.

"Nonsense," said Felicity. "It's Christmas Eve! There won't be a better time to bring some Christmas spirit to these poor stranded fairies."

"Unless we wait for next year?" suggested Holly hopefully.

"Come on!" said Felicity. "The screams sounded like they were coming from that house over there. Follow me!"

When they got to the house it was very quiet. The lights were on, but it appeared as though no one was in.

"This house gives me the creeps,"

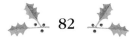

said Holly, who really was looking
for an excuse to go home and get
ready for the candlelit carol service.

The house was very tall and very
thin, quite unlike any of the houses
in Little Blossoming itself. Bravely,
Felicity knocked on the door with the
end of her wand. But her knocks were
met with silence.

"No answer!" said Felicity. "Perhaps
they've just popped out."

"In this weather?" said Polly, looking
around for signs of fairy life in the
snow.

"There's not another house here
with the lights on. There must be
someone in," said Daisy.

Felicity knocked again, even more
loudly this time. But there was still
no answer, so she bent down to call

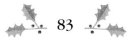

through the letter box. As she did so the door unexpectedly swung open on to an empty hallway, and a warm blast of air fell over the fairies.

"Let's get inside out of the cold!" said Holly, jumping through the door. "Hello!" she called out, a little nervously. "Is anyone home? We've come to bring you some Christmas magic!"

But the house was completely silent and still.

"You look on this floor," said Felicity to Daisy and Winnie, "and Holly, Polly and I will look upstairs."

"Isn't it a bit rude to wander around someone else's house without their permission?" asked Daisy conscientiously.

"We all heard those screams," said

Felicity. "Something might have happened to the fairies on this island, and we're the only ones here to help them."

* * *

It was strange to wander through a house that had no tree, presents or decorations to celebrate the special time of year.

Tentatively, Daisy and Winnie pushed open the doors on the ground floor one by one, but there were no fairies to be seen.

"I don't want to sound silly, but I feel like I'm being watched!" said Daisy.

"There were definitely some fairies here not long ago," said Winnie, picking up a half-drunk mug of hot chocolate that still felt warm.

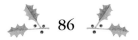

"But where have they gone?" asked
Daisy as she opened up the door to
the next room.

Felicity, Polly and Holly had had
no luck upstairs either. Each of the
four doors opened on to empty
rooms. But, like Daisy and Winnie,

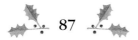

they had a sense that fairies had
been there not long before. Felicity
and the others were just about to
check the bathroom before heading
down when they heard a shriek from
the ground floor, closely followed by
loud screams… then suddenly
everything was silent.

"Quickly!" said Felicity, flying
downstairs at top speed. "That
sounded like Daisy and Winnie!"

But when they got to the floor
below there was no one there. Felicity,
Polly and Holly looked everywhere,
but in vain.

"I didn't like this before and I
certainly don't like it now," said Holly,
her wings quivering. "This is turning
out to be the worst Christmas Eve of
my life!"

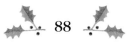

"Let's all split up," suggested Polly calmly. "They've got to be on this floor somewhere. Daisy and Winnie definitely didn't come upstairs and they would never have left without us."

So, while Polly went to look in the kitchen, Felicity stayed in the sitting room, and Holly walked round to the dining room, where she was sure the screams had come from.

It didn't take Felicity long to establish there was definitely no one in the sitting room, and she was just about to go to help Polly when she heard a quiet wail! As she leapt round the chair to dash into the kitchen, Felicity saw the half-drunk mug of hot chocolate. Quickly she picked it up and felt it was warm.

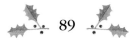

"Did you hear that, Polly?" she called out as she flew into the kitchen… but it was empty!

"Holly!" cried Felicity as she ran in to the dining room. "Is Polly with you? I've found half a mug of warm hot chocolate. There's definitely been someone h…"

Felicity's voice trailed off. The dining room was empty!

Felicity was beside herself. Then suddenly she saw a tiny piece of tinsel sticking out from between the doors of a large cupboard in the corner of the room. Slowly she walked over to inspect it more closely. It was the same tinsel Holly had been wearing around her neck like a scarf! Carefully she bent down and put her eye to the keyhole, and as she did so there was an enormous thump from inside the cupboard!

Without warning, the doors flew open, knocking Felicity from her feet and making her heart miss a beat.

"SURPRISE!" cried a dozen fairies as they tumbled unceremoniously into the room.

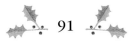

"We walked in on a game of sardines!" laughed Daisy, helping Felicity up.

"One person hides and then as

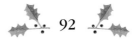

each person finds them, they join them in their hiding place, until there's only one person left looking, and that person was you!" giggled Holly.

"We had to do something to make us feel Christmassy!" said one of the other fairies that had fallen from the cupboard.

"Even if we don't have any Christmas decorations or presents, we realized we could still play Christmas party games!" said another.

∗ ∗ ∗

It took no time at all before Felicity, Holly, Polly, Daisy and Winnie had made lots of new friends and were having great fun playing the sorts of games that they usually only played after a large Christmas lunch. It was

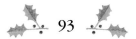

so much fun that the fairies didn't notice that the snow had stopped falling outside for the first time in days, and the sun was peeping out from behind the clouds.

"We really missed not seeing a Christmas show this year," said one of the island fairies. "Normally we all love to see a festive pantomime or ballet."

Felicity exchanged looks with her friends and grinned.

"Well, that's perfect," she said. "Because the reason we came to see you wasn't to play Christmas party games but to put on an ice show for you. We've got a Christmas pantomime you'll love!"

It didn't take the fairy friends long to put on their hilarious costumes

and featherweight wings, lace up
their ice skates, and skate on to the
lake to begin their routine. The island
fairies wrapped up warm and
watched in awe from the bank.

"Hurray!" cried the crowd after the
show had finished, running on to the
ice to hug the fairies. "That was
fantastic and so Christmassy!"

"Even though we've missed out on
all the usual things that make
Christmas magical, this has made up
for it!" said the smallest island fairy,
jumping up and down.

Just then there was an enormous
keeeerrrrrakk! Down the middle of
the ice there suddenly appeared the
most gigantic crack!

"Quick!" said Polly. "Hover!"

But Felicity, Holly, Winnie, Daisy

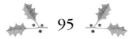

and Polly's featherweight wings were
no good for hovering.

"I can't!" said Felicity, the weight of her small body putting pressure on the ice.

"It's breaking up!" said Daisy, who was pulled into the air by one of the island fairies as the ice beneath her slowly broke apart.

Knowing that this was no time to conserve their wing power for warmth, the island fairies got Felicity and her friends safely on to the bank. Quietly they all watched in wonder as the ice broke up into huge slabs.

"Our boats!" cried one of the island fairies, spotting the bobbing vessels further down the lake. "They've been freed! Now the ice has gone, it means we can use them to get across to Little Blossoming!"

"Just in time for the candlelit carol

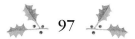

service," said Felicity, looking up at the stars that had begun to appear in the sky. "And to wish everyone a very magical Christmas!"

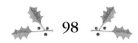

Christmas is a time
for spreading

lots of festive
fairy fun

Emma Thomson's
felicity Wishes®

Felicity decides to take a
summer job in a cinema, but things
don't quite go to plan in

Designer Drama

Cinema Collision

Polly had been waiting for Felicity Wishes to answer her front door for ages. When she bent over and peeped through the letter box, she couldn't believe her eyes. "What in Fairy World are you doing?" she called through the flap.

"Just coming!" strained Felicity sounding panicky.

When Felicity did finally open her door it was with her foot! Her arms were tied up in so much wool it had proved impossible to free herself completely.

Polly stood silently on the doorstep, dumbfounded.

"Come in, won't you," said Felicity pogoing ahead of her. "I had a bit of an accident, but I'm sorting it out now."

"What…?" was all Polly could say, when she saw the mountain of wool in Felicity's sitting room.

"I don't know what went wrong," said Felicity trying to free her arms. "Would you like to get yourself a drink… sorry to be a terrible host. I'd get you one myself only…"

"Only you're a bit tied up!" said Polly suddenly bursting out into fits of giggles. "Oh, Felicity! What are you like? If you tell me where I can find some scissors I can help get you out of this mess!"

Felicity pointed with her best ballet foot to the drawer in the large gold cupboard in the corner.

∗ ∗ ∗

Soon Felicity was free and the two of them were sitting around the kitchen table drinking strawberry milkshakes.

"I've just been so bored!" confided Felicity to her friend, "and it's only the first week of the holidays."

"Why don't you tidy your bedroom?" suggested Polly, who was always very practical.

"What's the point when it just gets messy again," said Felicity, slurping froth through her straw noisily.

"What about gardening? Why don't you plant some bulbs and tend to them as they grow?" said Polly.

Felicity dropped her straw. "You know I'm not like Daisy. I don't like getting my wand dirty, and there are always all those creepy crawlies."

"What about taking up a hobby, maybe making something?" suggested Polly, undeterred.

"You mean like knitting?" said Felicity, pulling several strands of wool from her hair.

"Maybe not," said Polly giggling, and reached over to pick up *The Daily Flutter* from the pile of magazines for inspiration.

"I know!" She said turning to the

back page and pointing. "Why don't you get a holiday job?"

"A job?" said Felicity frowning. "That doesn't sound like much fun to me."

"It could be doing anything though," said Polly, getting quite excited herself. "If I wasn't busy writing a book about teeth, I'd get a job during the holidays."

Polly wanted to be a Tooth Fairy. She was the most studious of all Felicity's friends and had set herself the task of writing a book about her favourite subject in her time off.

"Look!" she continued, "There's all sorts. Cinema attendants, waitresses, temporary Post Fairy positions, there's even a vacancy for a dental assistant," Polly said dreamily.

"Let me see," said Felicity, turning the paper to face her. "Hmm, cinema attendants give out ice-cream, don't they?" she said thoughtfully, "…and they get to watch the latest films all day!" she continued, her mind racing, "…and the only bit that could get boring would be showing people to their seats."

"But that's not boring," said Polly, trying to encourage her friend. "Just think of all the fairies you could meet, and all the friends you could make!"

That did it! Felicity's favourite thing in the whole world was making friends and she was known as being one of the friendliest fairies in Little Blossoming. The job of cinema attendant sounded perfect!

Without losing any time, Felicity carefully tore out the advert, picked up her wand and flew with Polly straight down to the cinema.

* * *

When she emerged from the cinema, Felicity was bouncing for joy!

"I got it!" she squealed, clapping her hands. "I got the job, and I start right away!"

"That's fantastic," said Polly who had been waiting anxiously for her friend. "Why don't we meet at Sparkles when you're finished and you can tell me all about it!"

"OK – see you later," called Felicity as she disappeared off to put on her new uniform.

* * *

Polly had arranged for Felicity's two other close friends, Holly and Daisy, to be in Sparkles, the café, when she finished the first day at her new job.

Holly spotted Felicity first and waved her wand frantically to catch her attention.

"Over here!" she called.

Felicity, head down, walked slowly towards their table.

"How did it go?" said Daisy excitedly. "Polly told us all about it! It sounds wonderful."

"Wonderful if you like scary monsters," said Felicity as she sat down.

"What do you mean?" said Polly confused. "I thought you were handing out ice-creams in the cinema and showing fairies to their seats."

Felicity picked up her hot chocolate to steady her shaking hands and only succeeded in spilling it all over the table. She burst into tears.

"Oh, I can't do anything right" she said.

Polly got up and gave her a hug. "Tell us all about it," she said softly.

"Everything began so magically," Felicity said, wiping away her tears. "My uniform was pink and white striped, which I was very happy about because it matched my favourite tights, and then they gave me the most enormous box of yummy ice-cream to hang around my neck!"

"It does sound wonderful," said Holly confused.

"And that wasn't all," continued Felicity. "Soon the whole cinema was full of fairies who were so nice."

"What happened?" said Daisy, putting down her mug.

"Well, I was so busy chatting and making friends, the film had already started by the time I got round to showing the fairies to their seats. It was dark, and even with my torch I kept tripping up. So did the fairies who'd come to see the film. There was popcorn and fizzy pop everywhere!"

"It's an easy mistake," said Polly, rubbing Felicity's arm. "It was dark."

"That's just what the manageress said when she heard all the commotion," continued Felicity, "which made me feel a bit better. But not for long. The film showing was a horror film, with big scary monsters. I couldn't look at the screen, and so instead I ended up staring at the ice-cream hanging around my neck. It looked so nice, and I thought it was probably important that I knew what all the flavours tasted like."

"You didn't eat it all?!" said Holly, clamping her hand over her mouth.

"I didn't mean to," said Felicity. "But somehow it just happened. There was none left in the interval for anyone else and everybody got very upset."

"Well, it's not a disaster, it was just your first day. I'm sure the manageress understood that it was really just a mistake."

"Well, no," said Felicity sheepishly. "It probably would have been OK. That is, if I hadn't been sick. All over isle G."

All three of Felicity's fairy friends groaned in despair and buried their faces in their hands.

The fairies finished up their hot chocolates and gave Felicity a lot of fairy hugs and encouragement for finding a new job, then went their separate ways home.

* * *

It was a week before they all met up again to see how Felicity had got on with her job-hunting but she didn't seem any happier.

"Well," began Felicity, looking very sorry for herself. "My job of Post Fairy started well. The Post Office offered me a job posting special letters in the afternoon. My first day went brilliantly. I had five letters and everyone I delivered them to ended up inviting me in for a cup of tea. That day I made five new friends."

"How lovely," said Daisy.

"It was the next day that everything went a bit wrong," continued Felicity. "I had twenty-five letters to post, and by the end of the day I had drunk ten cups of tea and had only posted nine letters."

"Ten teas and nine letters?" asked Holly confused.

"Yes, Miss Meandering the geography teacher had a lovely letter from a fairy friend in Russia, and I drank two cups of tea while she translated it for me."

"What did you do?" asked Polly concerned.

"Oh, the post mistress asked me to hand the undelivered letters back and said I should leave. She was very nice but she just didn't think my skills were suited to the job."

"I think you should try something artistic. You're so good at that sort of thing," suggested Daisy.

"Oh, I did that after the Post Fairy job," said Felicity. "I decided to make friendship bracelets for a shop in Bloomfield," and Felicity waggled her hand in front of her friends to show them one of her creations.

"That's lovely!" said Holly who was

always very fashionable. "The colours you've used are beautiful."

"And the detail in the tiny plaits you've woven must have taken ages," said Polly, carefully studying her friends bracelet.

"We'll all have to go to the shop in Bloomfield to get one," said Daisy, impressed.

Felicity pulled her hand away from her friends' gaze. "Well, there might be a problem with that."

Read the rest of

Emma Thomson's

felicity Wishes

Designer Drama

to find out if Felicity will ever
find the perfect summer job.

If you enjoyed this book, why not try
another of these fantastic story collections?

Designer Drama

Star Surprise

Clutter Clean-out

Newspaper Nerves

Enchanted Escape

Whispering Wishes

7
Sensational Secrets

8
Friends Forever

9
Happy Hobbies

10
Party Pickle

11
Wand Wishes

12
Dancing Dreams

13

Spooky Sleepover

14

Fashion Fiasco

15

Pink Paradise

16

Spectacular Skies

17

Dreamy Daisy

18

Perfect Polly

Winnie's Wonderland

Holly's Hideaway

Fairy Fun

Look out for these three special editions

Summer Sunshine

Christmas Calamity

Winter Wishes

Christmas Calamity

Summer Sunshine

Winter Wishes

Felicity Wishes shows you how to create your own sparkling style, throw a fairy sleepover party and make magical treats in this fabulous mini series. With top tips, magic recipes, fairy products and shimmery secrets.

Sleepover Magic

Cooking Magic

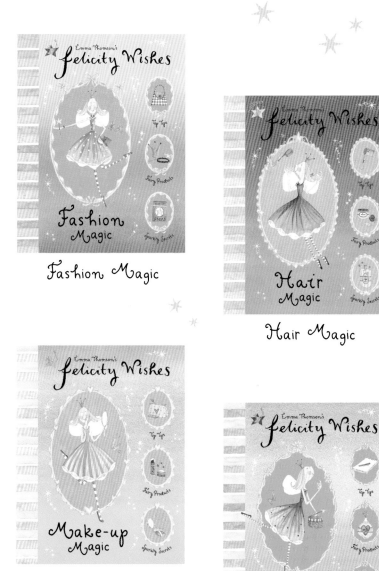

Fashion Magic

Hair Magic

Make-up Magic

Beauty Magic

CELEBRATE THE JOYS OF FRIENDSHIP WITH FELICITY WISHES!

Felicity Wishes always tries her best to make her friends dreams comes true.

Write in and tell us about a friend you think should be praised for her generosity, sense of fun, and kindness, and you could see your letter in one of Felicity Wishes' books.

Please send in your letters, including your name and age with a stamped self-addressed envelope to:

Felicity Wishes Friendship Competition

Hodder Children's Books, 338 Euston Road, London NW1 3BH

Australian readers should write to...

Hachette Children's Books
Level 17/207 Kent Street, Sydney, NSW 2000, Australia

New Zealand readers should write to...

Hachette Children's Books
PO Box 100-749 North Shore Mail Centre, Auckland, New Zealand

Closing date is 30 April 2007

ALL ENTRIES MUST BE SIGNED BY A PARENT OR GUARDIAN
TO BE ELIGIBLE ENTRANTS MUST BE UNDER 13 YEARS

For full terms and conditions visit www.felicitywishes.net/terms

Josie is my best friend because she is friendly to me and the people around me all the time. She also likes some of the things I like so we always have lots to talk about. Josie is my best friend because we never fall out so all the time we can we play with each other, she is loyal and we don't lie to each other or gossip about each other, we sit next to each other so we can see each other all the time. Josie also is my best friend because we help each other out all the time and we always stick up for each other

Bethan Metters age 11

WIN FELICITY WISHES PRIZES!

From January 2006, there will be a Felicity Wishes fiction book publishing each month (in Australia and New Zealand publishing from April 2006) with a different sticker on each cover. Collect all 12, stick them on the collectors' card which you'll find in *Dancing Dreams* or download from www.felicitywishes.net.

Send in your completed card to the relevant address below and you'll be entered into a monthly, grand prize draw to receive a Felicity Wishes prize.*

Felicity Wishes Collectors' Competition

Hodder Children's Books, 338 Euston Road, London NW1 3BH

Australian readers should write to...
Hachette Children's Books
Level 17/207 Kent Street, Sydney, NSW 2000

New Zealand readers should write to...
Hachette Children's Books
PO Box 100-749 North Shore Mail Centre, Auckland

*A draw to pick 50 winners each month will take place from January 2007 to 30th June 2007.

For full terms and conditions visit www.felicitywishes.net/terms

WOULD YOU LIKE TO BE
'A Friend of Felicity'?

Felicity Wishes has her very own website,
filled with lots of sparkly fairy fun and information
about Felicity Wishes and all her fairy friends.

Just visit:

www.felicitywishes.net

to find out all about
Felicity's books,
sign up to
competitions,
quizzes and
special offers.

And if you want
to show how much
you adore and admire
your friends, you can
even send them a
swish Felicity e-card
for free. It will truly
brighten up their day!

For full terms and conditions visit www.felicitywishes.net/terms